ANDROMON'S ATTACK

DIGITAL DIGIMON MONSTERS

J. E. BRIGHT

HarperEntertainment

An Imprint of HarperCollinsPublishers

HarperEntertainment
An Imprint of HarperCollins*Publishers*
10 East 53rd Street, New York, NY 10022

HarperCollins books are available at special quantity discounts for bulk purchases for sales promotions, premiums, or fund-raising. For information, please call or write: Special Markets Department, HarperCollins Publishers Inc., 10 East 53rd Street, New York, NY 10022. Telephone: (212) 207-7528. Fax: (212) 207-7222.

ISBN 0-06-107188-9

First printing: August 2000

Printed in the United States of America

Visit HarperEntertainment on the World Wide Web at
www.harpercollins.com

❖ 10 9 8 7 6 5 4 3 2

1

"We've passed this place before," Sora Takenouchi said. She stopped walking in the middle of a big green field, peering up at the blue sky decorated with white puffy clouds. Sora adjusted her hat as she stared at the familiar surroundings.

Joe Kido stopped beside Sora. "You mean we walked an entire circle all the way around the whole planet?" he asked, pushing up his glasses.

Joe, Sora, and the other five kids had been wandering around DigiWorld for days, ever since they'd been transported there by tiny

computer digivices. Those days had been jam-packed with dangerous adventures, and the kids had survived thanks to the protection of their new Digimon friends.

Mimi Tachikawa fell to her knees on the grass. "I can't walk that far, can I?" she moaned. "I'm so tired."

Beside Mimi, Takeru "T.K." Takaishi, the youngest of the kids, slumped to the grass and lay on his back. "My feet are hot," he whined.

Patamon, the Digimon who always hung out with T.K., fluttered his wings and landed on T.K.'s knees. Patamon's round body heaved as he panted exhaustedly.

Yamato Ishida, whom everybody called Matt, stopped next to T.K. and looked down at his younger brother. "I guess we're taking a break," Matt said.

"It's not like we have someplace to be," Sora said.

"I guess you're right," Taichi "Tai" Kamiya added. Tai tightened his goggles on his forehead so that they held up his wild spiky hair. "No reason to hurry."

Koushiro Izumi—better known as Izzy—

sat down on the grass and opened his lap-top computer. He began typing rapidly on its keyboard.

"Check out Izzy," Matt told the others. "He's probably trying to e-mail the aliens." One of Izzy's theories was that aliens had transported them to DigiWorld.

Tai smiled. "Maybe he's asking them to beam him up," he said.

After shaking his head, Izzy let out a big

sigh. "Still crashed," he muttered. "And the warranty expired."

"Hey, Izzy," Tai called, "I know how to get it to boot up." He grabbed the little computer out of Izzy's hands and gave it a good whack. "You've just got to give it a couple of subtle adjustments," he said.

"Hey!" Izzy shouted, trying to grab the computer back. "Are your brain cells malfunctioning?"

"Relax," Tai replied. "You would think I'm hurting the dumb thing." He shrugged and returned the computer to Izzy.

"Too bad your brain isn't as big as your hair," Sora put in. "Maybe Izzy doesn't want grimy fingerprints and dents all over his computer."

Tai looked annoyed at Sora's comment, but then his eyes widened as he noticed something odd on the other side of the field. "Hey!" he shouted. "Do you guys see smoke over there?"

Before anybody could answer, Tai dashed across the field. "I'll check it out!" he called.

Agumon, Tai's Digimon partner, chased after him. Agumon looked sort of like a shrunken dinosaur. "Hey, wait for me," he yelled.

Joe, the oldest of the kids, shook his head. "Tai's got the attention span of a gnat," he said.

"Ah, whatever," Matt replied.

"Huh!" Izzy said, without looking up from his computer. "It's working again.

We've got graphics, we've got sound. . . ." He typed for a moment, checking out the computer's systems. "Beautiful," he announced. "It's up and running."

Then Izzy noticed a flashing lightning-bolt symbol in the corner of his screen. "But it indicates that the battery needs recharging," he explained. "That's odd."

"Get over here!" Tai yelled. "Quick!"

The kids and the Digimons jumped to their feet and raced across the green grass to where Tai and Agumon waited. From that part of the field, they all could see the edge of a sloping hill where thin ribbons of yellowish

smoke wriggled in the air. The tips of smokestacks poked over the crest of the hill.

Everybody ran closer for a better view. As they neared, an enormous grayish-blue-and-yellow building appeared. The huge rectangular structure was covered with chimneys and giant pipes. A haze of gray smoke made the building seem bleak and dangerous.

"It looks like some sort of factory," Joe declared.

Matt nodded. "Let's hope they can manufacture a way for us to get home."

2

"I wonder what they make in there?" Joe asked as the group headed for the factory.

Mimi giggled. "I don't know," she replied, "but wouldn't it be great if there's a manu-facturer's outlet store? They always have killer deals!"

After a short walk, the kids and the

Digimons found themselves inside the building. They wandered through shiny metal passageways, listening to their footsteps echo in the empty halls.

"There doesn't seem to be anyone here," Matt said.

Sora paused in front of a system of giant turning gears, peering around at the vast pipes lining the ceiling. "There's got to be someone running the equipment," she pointed out.

"I don't know," Izzy said. He waved his hand at the spinning gears. "It appears to be doing quite well all by itself."

T.K. stopped to watch a long assembly line. As the belt moved, robotic arms and hands added pieces of machinery to strange objects sliding down the line. On the top of each object, an arm placed a twisty antenna.

"Matt," T.K. asked his older brother, "what are these machines making?"

"You got me," Matt replied. "Maybe parts for robots or space ships."

The gang kept walking until they came

out of a maze of passageways into a large open space over a grate. The room was crisscrossed with high catwalks. They hurried across the grate and pushed open a door on the far wall.

"Hello!" Tai called as he stepped inside. "Is anybody here?"

Everybody stared in awe when they saw what was inside. A giant battery stretched up to the ceiling, glowing faintly in a pastel pink-and-blue electrical haze.

"We found the Power Room," Tai said.

Izzy couldn't take his eyes off the giant battery. "A battery like that could run my computer forever," he said. "I wonder if there's a way to access its power."

After a few minutes of watching Izzy inspect the battery, Tai got bored with waiting around. He opened another door and stepped through, followed by Sora and Joe, and their Digimon partners—Agumon, Biyomon, and Gomamon. Matt, Mimi, T.K., and their Digimon friends stayed behind to help Izzy.

Tai, Joe, and Sora walked down a long hall. Suddenly, they heard a creepy metallic groan from down the passageway.

"Did you hear that?" Biyomon asked.

"Yeah," Joe replied nervously.

At the end of the hall, Tai pushed open another door.

Sora and Joe gasped.

Spread out on the floor in front of them was a pile of shiny junk. Under the mix of metal barrels and gears, a bizarre steel creature was pinned to the ground.

"What do you suppose happened to him?" Tai asked.

Sora shrugged. "I don't know," she replied, "but let's see if we can help."

Tai leaned forward for a better look. The creature had long metal arms and legs and glowing red eyes. "It's just a busted robot," he said.

"It's not a robot," Gomamon said, flapping his furry flippers. "It's Andromon."

"What?" Tai asked. "This big klunk is a Digimon?"

"Yes," Agumon told his friend. He nodded his lizardlike snout. "And he's very much advanced."

Biyomon waved her feathered wings.

"Poor thing," she said. "I guess he got mangled in the gears."

"Maybe if we work together, we can pull him out of there," Sora said.

Sora and Tai each grabbed one of Andromon's cold metal legs and pulled as hard as they could. The gears shifted around with a screech.

"I think it's moving!" Tai shouted as he pulled.

"Hey—something's happening," Joe pointed out. "He's coming loose!"

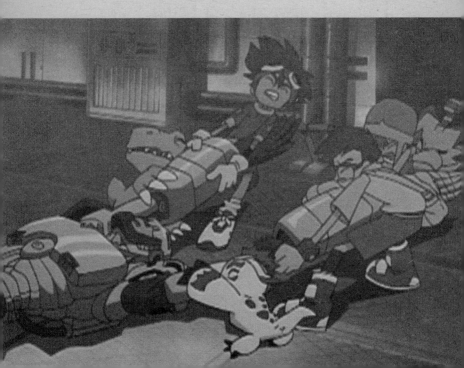

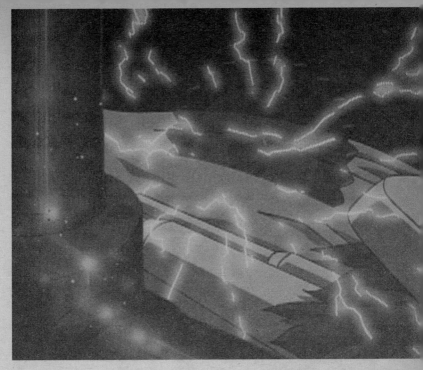

As Andromon slid away from the pile of junk, one of the gears—a black one—slid into the Digimon's leg and vanished beneath its metal casing.

Joe, Sora, and Tai let out a happy cheer as the barrels rolled off Andromon.

Agumon peered down into Andromon's steel face. "I think he's slowly coming to," he said.

"He just needs a couple of whacks for a jump start!" Tai decided, but Sora and Joe held him back before he could pound on the dazed Digimon.

Andromon's eyes glowed more brightly as he sat up.

"Um," Joe said nervously, "I saw a movie once where a robot came to life and ate everybody. . . ."

Sora laughed. "He looks friendly enough," she told Joe. "I'm sure if we're nice to him, he'll be nice to us—"

Andromon jumped to his feet with a

clang, looming high above the kids. Then he reached down and grabbed Sora by the leg. Sora screamed as Andromon yanked her far above the floor and held her upside down.

Sora dangled from Andromon's firm grip. "Forget what I said about him being friendly!" she yelled.

3

"I shall punish alien intruders!" Andromon bellowed. He shook Sora until she let out a scream.

"Andromon is one of the most powerful Digimons of all," Gomamon said. "His body is a tireless machine capable of almost anything!"

"I don't want to find out what he's capable of doing to Sora!" Tai shouted. "Let's attack him with all we've got!"

Biyomon narrowed her eyes. "Spiral Twister!" she hollered, flapping her white-and-pink wings. A green spiral of energy swirled out of Biyomon and sizzled against Andromon's head.

The big robotic Digimon was stunned for a moment. Biyomon's blast wasn't enough

to knock him out, but he dropped Sora, then let out a fierce howl of rage.

Sora fell and crashed into Tai and Joe, who cushioned her fall.

Andromon clanked his way toward them, his red eyes glowing with dangerous anger.

"Uh . . . Agumon?" Tai asked. "How about blasting the ceiling?"

Agumon let out a grunt of agreement. With a roar, an orange ball of flame shot

out of his mouth. The fireball blazed into the ceiling and exploded, loosening dozens of metal support beams.

The steel bars crashed on Andromon, knocking him down with a big clang. Groaning, he struggled against the heavy beams, but he couldn't pull himself free.

"He's going to have one ugly headache," Tai said.

Sora nodded. "No doubt," she agreed.

"Now let's get out of here," Joe said.

The three kids and their Digimon friends hurried away from Andromon, heading deeper into the factory.

Meanwhile, in the Power Room, Izzy and Tentomon examined the tall walls of the giant battery. Mimi, Matt, T.K., and their Digimon partners, Palmon, Gabumon, and Patamon, had wandered off to the next room to watch the nonstop assembly line create its mysterious mechanical objects. Izzy was much more interested in inspecting the battery.

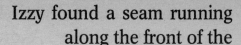

Izzy found a seam running along the front of the battery's curved side. "Aha!" he exclaimed. "I've located an access panel to the interior operations!" Izzy tugged on the panel and a hidden door in the battery's wall swung open.

"Ooh," Tentomon whispered. He waved his beetle arms in the air, staring in amazement at what was inside.

The interior of the battery was circular and hollow like a farm silo. The walls were made of a rare metal that flickered with pastel pink-and-blue misty energy. Strange black symbols were written in a unknown language over every inch of the radiant walls.

Izzy stepped inside, excited to check out the eerie shapes and squiggles.

"What exactly do you think this is?"

Tentomon asked. His high-pitched buzz of a voice sounded worried.

"These markings appear to be some type of binary annotations," Izzy decided. "It's a computer program!"

Izzy reached out and dragged his finger

against one of the symbols. "A very complicated program, indeed," he said.

The black letter wiped clean under Izzy's finger, and the lights flickered off all over the factory.

*　　*　　*

A few rooms away from where they had pinned Andromon, Tai, Sora, and Joe found a long tunnel, which they hoped led back to the other kids. They panted as they sprinted down the narrow hall, followed closely by Agumon, Biyomon, and Gomamon.

The tunnel, too dank and too narrow for comfort to begin with, became positively terrifying when the lights went out.

Stopping short, the group clung together in the bluish darkness. "I break out in hives in the dark," Joe whimpered.

A clank echoed in the inky distance.

"What was that?" Joe demanded.

"I hope it wasn't Andromon," Sora said. "Could he have gotten free?"

Tai shifted on his feet nervously. "It might be a good plan to keep on moving so we don't find out," he replied.

"I'm for that," Joe said.

But nobody moved. The blacked-out tunnel was too scary and no one wanted to rush down it blindly.

Sora screamed as a pair of glowing red eyes appeared in the darkness.

"Intruders sighted!" Andromon announced robotically. "And I don't like intruders!"

Andromon's metal armor shimmered into view. "Lightning Blade!" he yelled. He conjured up a blue boomerang made out of pure energy and hurled it. It blasted down the hall toward the kids.

Tai, Sora, Joe, and their Digimons took off running in the opposite direction, into the tunnel's black void.

Izzy stood in the darkened interior of the giant battery with Tentomon. Only the gentle glow of the electrical current in the walls allowed them to see each other. "Do you suppose I could have deleted the wrong program?" Izzy asked.

"I think that's a distinct possibility," Tentomon replied. "Why don't you try to *un*delete it?"

"Not a bad idea," Izzy said. He reached into his jacket and took out a slim silver pen. Izzy pulled off the cap and showed the pen to Tentomon. "I've got black metallic ink right here," he said. Then he peered at the dimly lit symbols, focusing on the spot he had wiped clean. "A stroke right here should do it. . . ."

As soon as Izzy fixed up the smudge, the overhead lights flashed back on.

"There we go!" Izzy announced with a smile.

When the lights came on, Tai, Joe, Sora, and their Digimon partners ran even faster.

As they raced away from Andromon and across a rickety catwalk high above the floor, the six friends tried not to panic. The robot Digimon was hot on their heels, his red eyes blazing.

"I don't like this at all!" Joe wailed.

"Lightning Blade!" Andromon shouted. Again, a brilliant blue boomerang appeared, sending off showers of sparks. "And fire!"

Joe, Tai, and Sora shrieked in terror as the boomerang whizzed down the catwalk, heading straight for them.

"Jump!" Tai hollered.

The kids and the Digimons threw themselves over the catwalk's railing, three on each side. They held on tightly to the metal banisters, dangling over the sheer drop.

The Lightning Blade blazed between them, missing completely.

Andromon let out a furious roar. "Hear me, intruders!" he thundered. "Andromon will exact his vengeance!"

Tai clung to the catwalk's railing. "Hey!"

he shouted at Andromon. "Come on! We're the ones who jump-started you, remember?"

Back inside the humongous battery, Izzy's computer began beeping. "Huh?" Izzy murmured.

"Look at the screen!" Tentomon exclaimed. "It's acting rather strangely."

Izzy stared at the display. Each line of code shifted around, sliding across the screen until all the words were jumbled. Then the mess of graphics blurred into a

whirling shape in the middle of the screen.

Another tiny computer strapped to Izzy's wrist like a digital watch began to hum and pulse with lights. "And my digivice has been activated as well!" Izzy announced.

Tentomon hunched over to peer at Izzy's laptop computer. "That shape that's spinning there," he asked, "is it a map?"

"I believe it's pure information," Izzy replied. "This is merely scientific speculation, but I believe I've stumbled onto something more than just a computer game. And I'm about to abandon my alien theory as well."

Before Izzy could explain more, Tentomon hopped up and down, wriggling his antennae. Yellow lightning flashed along his chest armor. "Oh, my, it's getting hot in here!" Tentomon cried. "Ow! Ow! I'm burning up! Do something, quickly—I'm being zapped!"

The pressure begins to build on Joe when
the kids visit a factory that
doesn't make ANYTHING!

"I'm sure if we're nice to Andromon, he'll be nice to us–"

"I'm dancing like I've never danced before!"

"You puny ones dare to challenge Andromon?"

Greymon gets a little carried away sometimes.

Kabuterimon to the rescue!

Electro Shocker!

Numemons' numesludge attack.
Yuck!

"It's a happy day in Toy Town . . ."

. . . but not for the Numemons or the kids and their Digimons.

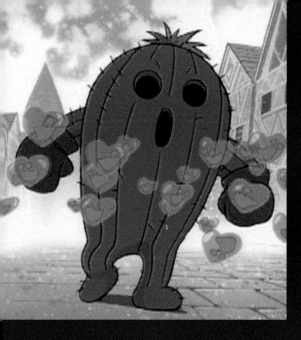

Palmon may be a lady, but she's no pushover! Especially when she digivolves to Togemon!

Monzaemon is a good Digimon when he's not infected with a Black Gear.

Hearts Attack! With a hug!

"What's going on?" Izzy asked, his eyes wide.

Lightning danced all around Tentomon. Smoke began to pour out of his shell as he jiggled around. "Ouch, I can't stand it!" he screamed. "I'm dancing like I've never danced before! Ow!"

Izzy glanced at his flashing digivice, and then at the mysterious swirling shape on his laptop. "Are they short-circuiting?" he wondered. "I'll have to cut the power." With a deep sigh, he pushed the power button on his laptop. "I never figured the mystery out," Izzy groaned. "Oh, well."

Tentomon slid to the ground as the computer went blank and the digivice and lightning stopped flashing.

"Ohhh," Tentomon moaned, slumping forward. "I don't like computers."

*　　*　　*

"Andromon will exact his vengeance!" the steel Digimon bellowed.

Tai was fed up with being pushed around. "Oh, yeah?" he hollered at Andromon. "Just try it, you tin can!"

As Andromon clomped down the catwalk, Tai let go of the railing. He dropped into the seat of a machine that looked like a crane. Tai pulled and pushed two big levers on the machine. High above the catwalk, the long neck of the crane swiveled, swinging a hook on a stout wire.

"Well?" Tai yelled at Andromon. "Come on!"

"Would you please stop taunting the deranged android?" Agumon begged Tai.

But Tai ignored his Digimon friend. He shifted the levers until the hook swung toward Andromon. "Yeah!" Tai cheered.

Just as Andromon was about to grab Sora, the hook snagged him on his back. Tai quickly pulled a lever and Andromon was hoisted high on the end of the crane.

Andromon groaned as he hung above the

32

catwalk. "Ground interrupt!" he announced in a robotic voice. "Altitude reading abnormal!"

Tai climbed back onto the catwalk and helped pull his friends up from where they were dangling. Then they all rushed off the catwalk before Andromon could free himself.

After all, it wouldn't take long for Andromon to cut the hook's cord with a blast from his Lightning Blade.

5

Izzy hurried out of the giant battery, searching for T.K., Matt, and Mimi. He found them by the assembly line, watching the mechanical arms taking apart the objects they'd just built.

"Hey, everybody!" Izzy called. "You'll never guess what I discovered!"

"What's up?" Matt asked.

"Get this," Izzy said. "The computer program operating this factory is producing the generating power to keep it going. Even more bizarre, in DigiWorld, basic data and simple information are living, viable substances!"

"What does that mean?" T.K. asked.

"It's alive," Izzy explained simply.

"Hey, guys!" Tai yelled as he ran full-speed into the room, followed by Sora, Joe, and their Digimons. "Listen up!"

"This doesn't sound like good news," Matt muttered.

"We've got to get out of here!" Tai shouted. "Now!"

"What do you mean, Tai?" Matt asked.

As if in answer, Andromon burst up through the floor. He climbed through the mess of broken tile to stand in front of the conveyor belt.

The kids screamed in fear.

"Capture intruders!" Andromon thundered. "Sensors detect hostility!"

Mimi smiled at Andromon. "Excuse me, Mr. Android," she asked politely, "but are you talking to us?"

"Bring intruders into firing range," Andromon continued. A panel flipped

open on his chest, revealing two tubes. "Bring missiles to position," Andromon said. "And fire!"

Two rockets launched out of Andromon's chest. They had saw-blade metallic grins on the fronts of their bodies and looked like vicious robotic fish.

The kids and their Digimons scattered, rushing to the sides.

T.K. didn't move as quickly as the others. He froze directly in the path of the missiles. "Help, Matt!" T.K. cried.

"T.K.!" Matt screamed.

Gabumon jumped in front of T.K. "Gabu-mon digivolve to . . . Garurumon!" the Rookie Digimon hollered.

The entire DigiWorld seemed to flash and warp as Matt's digivice began to pulse. Gabumon usually looked like a soft and cute white tiger cub with a rhinoceros horn and kangaroo legs. But as lights and digital particles exploded around him, he quickly transformed into a much bigger and stronger creature—Garurumon! Now he looked like a

mix between a fully grown white wolf and a
fierce eagle, only without any wings.

With his claw, Garurumon kicked the
missiles away from T.K. They spiraled into
the air, trailing smoke.

"Yipe!" T.K. cried.

But the missiles weren't destroyed. They
circled around, and when they had locked
on to the kids, the missiles' bear-trap
mouths popped open.

Agumon dashed to one side. "Agumon
digivolve to . . . Greymon!" he yelled.

Tai's digivice glowed and
DigiWorld shook and
trembled. Agumon
changed from a
cute yellow-and-
orange dinosaur
creature into a
full-size dino-
saur Digimon
that looked like
a *Tyrannosaurus
rex* with the head

38

of a triceratops. To make Greymon even more fearsome, he wore a black helmet over his face.

With a flick of Greymon's muscular tail, he smashed the missiles to the ground. Then both Greymon and Garurumon rushed Andromon from either side.

But they missed Andromon and smacked into each other, toppling to the floor.

"You puny ones dare to challenge me?"

Andromon bellowed. "Lightning Blade!" Andromon's terrifying boomerang weapon blazed across the room, striking Garurumon. Garurumon howled in pain.

Greymon launched a huge Nova Blast, which swirled flames around Andromon.

Andromon seemed more surprised than hurt by the blast.

But the attack gave Garurumon a moment to recover. He opened his mouth and launched his Howling Blaster. Andromon kicked at the flames, swirling them harmlessly around him.

"He's more powerful than either of our Digimons!" Matt exclaimed.

Sora climbed onto a wall for a better view. "Maybe it's because he's all machine," she said. "It's like he's digivolved far beyond the others."

"Is it possible we could lose?" Tai asked worriedly.

Andromon picked up Greymon and tossed him into Garurumon. The giant Digimons tumbled in a heap.

"He's beaten them both now," Tai said.

"It looks like there's no hope," Matt added sadly.

Tentomon tapped on Izzy's shoulder with one of his long, thin legs. "Re-enter that program that activated your digivice," he suggested.

"What for?" Izzy asked.

"I believe that's the key to my digivolution," Tentomon replied.

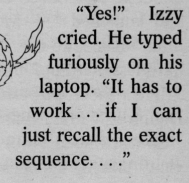

"Yes!" Izzy cried. He typed furiously on his laptop. "It has to work . . . if I can just recall the exact sequence. . . ."

On the screen, the lines shifted around again. The same bizarre shape whirled in the center of the display, and Izzy's digivice flashed.

Tentomon sizzled with lightning. But this time the effect didn't hurt him. Instead it filled him with transforming power.

Tentomon raised his insectoid legs above his head. "Tentomon digivolve to . . . Kabuterimon!" he shouted.

In a storm of energy, the cheerful beetle-like Digimon shed his friendly red and gray colors. He morphed into a frightening blue, yellow, and gray combination of a dragonfly and a lizard, standing on his hind legs. He had four sharp wings and four very strong-looking arms. Tentomon became a sleek fighting machine—Kabuterimon!

"We cracked the program!" Izzy cheered.

Kabuterimon barreled headlong toward Andromon. He slammed into the metallic Digimon, pushing him away from Greymon and Garurumon.

Andromon staggered, but quickly regained his balance. "Deploy armored missiles!" he yelled as the panel opened on his chest again.

"Doesn't that thing ever run out of gas?" Joe asked.

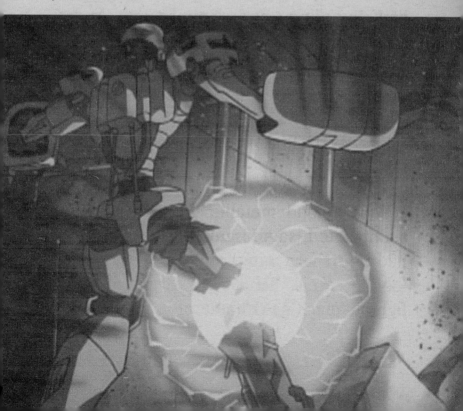

"That's it!" Izzy exclaimed. He peered over at Andromon's legs. One was different from the other—the right one wasn't encased in a metal shell.

"Hey, Kabuterimon!" Izzy yelled. "Cut his power! Demobilize his right leg and we'll interrupt his energy source!"

Kabuterimon nodded. "Electro Shocker!" he shouted.

Before Andromon could fire his missiles, a blistering blast of electricity surged out of Kabuterimon and slammed into Andromon's right leg. Andromon roared and nearly fell over.

Then the Black Gear slid out of Andromon's leg and whizzed into the air. The kids gasped as it exploded overhead like fireworks.

"That's wicked," Tai said.

With a loud metallic *thunk*, Andromon slumped to his hands and knees.

A few minutes later, the kids and the Digimons gathered around Andromon. Andromon sat up and smiled at everybody.

"That Black Gear reprogrammed my system somehow," he said apologetically. Even his voice sounded nicer now. "I'm normally a nonviolent Digimon."

"You could have fooled us," Tai replied.

"No kidding," Sora added.

Andromon shook his head sadly. "I never meant to hurt anyone," he whispered.

"Don't give it another thought," Matt said. "We all make mistakes."

"I can be of some help," Andromon said, his eyes glowing. "The best way to escape from this factory is to follow the underground waterway." He pointed over

to a chute in a far wall. "The labyrinth begins just beyond that point."

"Thanks, Andromon," Tai said.

Andromon smiled. "I hope that you find your way home," he said solemnly. "And, no matter what, please try to remember the big guy who turned out not to be so bad."

Tai returned the giant steel Digimon's grin. "There's one thing you can count on," Tai promised. "We'll never forget you, Andromon."

After everyone had said good-bye to Andromon, they set off down the chute. The small tunnel led to an enormous stinky sewer pipe. The walls of the pipe were curved and extremely green and slimy. A stream of bluish water flowed down the middle of the sewer, and wide stone paths stretched into the distance on either side of the waterway.

The kids were quiet for a while as they marched alongside the smelly stream. Finally, Joe broke the silence. "Am I the only one who finds strolling through the sewers the slightest bit disgusting?" he asked.

Sora let out a short scream, followed by a sad whimper.

"I don't know if it's *that* disgusting," Joe said quickly.

"Sora, are you all right?" Tai asked.

"Water fell from up there," Sora explained.

"That made you scream?" Izzy asked.

"Yeah," Sora replied. "Well, no. Uh . . . I miss having clean clothes," she said. "I loved doing laundry, letting the sunshine dry my clothes naturally—I miss that."

"It's okay to miss your home, Sora," Biyomon said. "Tai, what do you miss?"

"I miss playing sports," Tai said, "then taking a nice hot bath."

"I miss video games," T.K. put in. "I wasn't far from beating Matt."

"Beating me, T.K.?" Matt exclaimed. "I don't think so! Maybe in your dreams, kiddo!"

"So you don't miss anything from home, Matt?" Gabumon asked.

"Well, actually, now that you mention it," Matt began, "I've been dreaming about Mom's special Sunday meal for us . . .

grilled steaks! Mmm. Makes my mouth water!"

"I miss doing my homework," Joe said. "If I fall too far behind, I'll never get into a good college."

"I don't miss school," Mimi chirped. "But I do miss going on vacation! Nothing beats having a cool drink on a summer

day at the beach. I just love the ocean
air!"

"Wow, Mimi," T.K. said, "that sounds like
fun!"

"It is!" Mimi replied.

"Get a grip," Izzy said. "I miss accessing satellites through my computer to look at the stars and planets."

All the kids heaved big sighs.

"They really do come from another world," Agumon whispered to Gabumon.

"That's why they're depressed," Gabumon realized.

"Poor kids," Gomamon added.

A bizarre noise suddenly filled the sewer tunnel. It sounded like distant gobbles and slurps.

"Shh!" Tentomon instructed. "Listen, everyone—"

"Numemons!" Gabumon exclaimed nervously.

"Numemons?" Matt asked. "What are they?"

"They're really disgusting Digimons," Gomamon replied. "They live down here in the sewers."

"That's gross!" Tai said.

Tentomon nodded. "And so are they," he said.

"Are they big and strong?" T.K. asked, sounding worried.

"No, they're weak but smelly," Agumon replied. "Just wait until they get closer."

"What do you say we leave?" Joe suggested. "Or am I the only one who doesn't want to get

stomped by stinky sewer dwellers?"

"It's too late!" T.K. cried.

Dozens of small creatures appeared hopping and bobbing down the giant pipe. They were gross green blobs with round eyeballs on the top of antennae. Their disgusting tongues hung out of their mouths, and they slobbered constantly.

"There are too many of them," Agumon shouted. "Hurry, run!"

7

The Numemons chased the kids and their friends down the sewer tunnel.

"If they're not strong," Tai panted as he ran, "why do we have to run from them?"

"You'll see," Agumon promised. "Now run faster!"

The leader of the Numemons had a high goofy voice. "Let 'em have it!" he ordered.

The Numemons chucked chunks of a slimy pink substance at the kids. It stank horribly and corroded whatever it touched.

"They're throwing numesludge!" Biyomon warned.

"We've got to get out of here!" Joe shouted.

T.K. skidded to a stop when he noticed an upward-sloping turnoff in the sewer wall. "This way!" he shouted.

The kids and the Digimons took the sharp

turn, rushing up the side tunnel.

The Numemons didn't stop hurling their vile nume-sludge as they followed the kids up the tight passage.

Up ahead of the kids was the glow of sunlight—an exit to the outside!

When the Numemons hit the sunlight, they all bumped into each other, groaning and moaning.

"Why are they stopping?" Tai asked.

"The only thing that drives them away is sunlight," Agumon explained.

Tai let out a long relieved sigh.

Outside the tunnel they found blue sky, a grassy field, and rolling hills. The kids wandered into the field, thrilled to be out of the sewer.

"What's that twinkling over there?" Mimi asked. Everybody hurried closer and saw a small area covered with big rectangular metal boxes.

"Wow!" Mimi squealed. "Snack machines!

There must be thousands of them!"

"Or maybe just fifty," Izzy amended.

"How did they get here?" T.K. asked.

"Who cares?" Mimi replied. "There are so many snacks to choose from!"

"Mimi, they probably don't work," Tai reminded her. "Don't you remember the phone booths?" When the kids had first arrived in DigiWorld, they found some telephones, but they only had joke recordings playing on them. Nobody could make any calls.

"That's right," Palmon agreed. "I'll bet it's a trick, Mimi."

"I won't accept that!" Mimi insisted. She set off toward the vending machines.

Palmon groaned and then quickly followed.

When Mimi reached the rows of snack machines, she ducked down an aisle between them until she found an interesting one. "Yeah, soda!" she cheered. Mimi pulled coins out of her pocket. "You want a soda, too?" she asked Palmon.

"No, I don't!" Palmon snapped.

"You don't have to bite my head off," Mimi protested. She dropped a coin into the soda machine's slot.

Mimi screamed as the front of the vending machine fell open like a trap door.

Inside was the leader of the Numemons.

"Hey, cutie pie," he said cheerfully. "Let me take you out on a date!"

"He likes you!" Palmon teased.

"What?" Mimi exclaimed. "I wouldn't go near that short, slimy, sewer-sliding sludge slinger!"

"Quiet, Mimi," Palmon urged. "Don't make him mad."

"Who cares?" Mimi replied. "Besides, we're safe in the sunlight–"

Without warning, a bank of thick clouds rolled in front of the sun. The field got darker and colder instantly.

"How dare you call me *short*!" the Numemon leader demanded. "The date's off!" He rushed at Mimi, waving his arms and waggling his drooling tongue.

"Ack!" Mimi screamed. "Run!"

"Party time!" the Numemon leader yelled.

All around Mimi and Palmon, the vending machines popped open. Inside each one was a slobbery Numemon. They jumped out and sprinted toward Mimi and Palmon.

"Run!" Palmon screamed. "Get away!"

Mimi took off up the hill toward her friends, numesludge raining down around her.

As the slimy green sea of Numemons poured up the hill, all the other kids and Digimons followed Mimi in her rush across the field, away from the moldy monsters.

"Run! They're gaining!" Tai yelled.

"Let's split up!" Matt recommended.

Tai immediately began to veer away from him. "Yeah!" he agreed.

Numesludge plopped around the kids as they separated into three running groups.

The leader of the Numemon bounced after Mimi. He was backed up by a third of his creepy friends. "Heartbreaker!" the leader shouted.

Palmon and Mimi headed for a thick patch of forest. They ran into the woods, ducking behind trees to avoid being trashed with numesludge. Mimi hunched down behind a bush, and Palmon took shelter behind an oak.

"Come on out!" the leader shouted. Then he threw a big pile of numesludge against Palmon's tree.

Palmon jumped out from her hiding place and faced the slobbering Digimon with determination. She had a fierce scowl for a creature who basically looked like a walking onion. "Poison Ivy!" she shouted.

The Numemons squealed in fear. They hopped away frantically, vanishing in the woods.

Mimi ran out from behind her bush. "Palmon, thank you!" she chirped.

"But Mimi," Palmon protested, "I didn't do anything! Why'd they run?"

An explosion shook the woods. Mimi and Palmon lurched forward as a big cloud of pale red dust billowed up behind them.

Mimi gasped. Above her, as tall as the tops of the trees, was the biggest teddy bear Mimi had ever seen. He was bright yellow

and cheerful-looking, with the hint of a smile on his mouth.

"That's Monzaemon!" Palmon said.

When Monzaemon spoke, his deep scary voice vibrated the leaves on the trees. "Come visit us at Toy Town!" he ordered.

"Palmon," Mimi whispered. "Is he a Digimon, too?"

"Yes," Palmon replied. "He's in charge of a special place called Toy Town. There he takes care of all the abandoned Digimon toys, who love him."

"Is he harmless?" Mimi asked nervously.

"He always has been," Palmon replied.

"I must say, I'm so pleased to make your acquaintance!" Monzaemon boomed again. Then his eyes glowed intensely red, and two laser beams shot out from them. The beams seared into the ground right in front of Mimi and Palmon. They took off running.

"Acquaintance?" Mimi cried. "He's attacking us!"

"You think?" Palmon added sarcastically.

Monzaemon stomped after them between

the trees. His every footstep felt like a mini earthquake. "Please, come spend a fun day at Toy Town!" he thundered. Monzaemon kept shooting laser beams from his eyes, scarring the ground. "Why are you running?" he bellowed. "Did I startle you? Sorry!"

"Something's wrong," Palmon panted as she ran. "He's never acted like this before!"

"He does now!" Mimi screamed.

Mimi and Palmon burst out of the woods, back into the green field beyond.

The leader of the Numemon popped up from behind a tuft of grass. "Come here, cookie," he called to Mimi. "I'll protect you!"

"No, thanks!" Mimi shot back.

Palmon skidded to a halt. "Until we find the others we need him!" she reminded Mimi. Mimi stopped, too, and nodded with a sigh. Then she and Palmon jumped into the deep hole that the leader was hiding in. They pressed up against the dirt wall of the hole as Monzaemon took a giant stride over them.

"How about a kickin' game of soccer?" Monzaemon boomed. But he passed above Mimi, Palmon, and the Numemon leader without spotting them cowering below.

After a few moments, Mimi could no longer feel the thunder of his footsteps. "He's gone," she decided.

"Something bad must've happened in Toy Town," Palmon said as they climbed out of the hole and stood in the empty field.

The Numemon leader rubbed up against Mimi like a warty wet kitten. "Since I saved you, now will you go out with me?" he asked.

"No," Mimi replied. "Come on, let's go to Toy Town!"

"But the others—" Palmon began. Mimi took off running, so Palmon followed after her without finishing her sentence.

"Wow, she's so feisty!" the Numemon leader shouted. "What a girl!"

Mimi jogged through the woods in the direction Monzaemon had come from. It didn't take long for her and Palmon to find Toy Town. They saw it glowing through the forest, the tops of its pink-and-blue turrets

poking above the trees. Mimi and Palmon hurried to the front entrance.

"Wow, it really looks beautiful!" Mimi said. "Kind of like . . . a big amusement park!"

As they wandered through the streets of Toy Town, Mimi and Palmon gaped in awe at the old-fashioned homes and businesses lining the sidewalks. Tall towers shone like gems on top of the homes, and happy-faced bear balloons drifted in a rainbow of colors. But the streets were eerily quiet.

"It doesn't look like anyone's here," Mimi said.

Palmon glanced around worriedly. "Something's not right, Mimi," she replied.

As they paused in a town square, Tai burst out of a side street. He was running hard, and he had a fake smile plastered on his face. A tiny toy car zoomed after him. "Oh, boy this is fun!" Tai shouted as he ran from the wind-up car chasing him. "This is really fun!"

"That doesn't look like a lot of fun," Mimi said. She whirled around as Sora bolted across the square behind her.

A toy monkey clanging together cymbals tottered quickly after Sora. "This is so exciting, this is really exciting!" Sora yelled.

"What's going on here?" Palmon wondered.

Joe dashed through the town square. After every few steps, a giant plastic bird bobbed after him, nearly pecking him in the head

with its beak. "This really rocks!" Joe hollered. "Forget books! This really rocks!"

"Everyone sounds like a bunch of zombies," Mimi told Palmon.

"They do," Palmon said.

"Oh, well," Mimi chirped as they began to walk again. "They always were a little weird."

"I wish I knew what was going on here,"

Palmon muttered. "It's kind of creepy."

As they were passing a window of one of the stores, Mimi heard a rattling noise coming from inside.

"Hello!" yelled Agumon's voice. "Can

anyone hear us out there? Tai? Matt? Get us out of here!"

"It's coming from in there," Palmon said, pointing to the store window.

Mimi peered through the glass. She saw a medium-size trunk sitting in the middle of the floor, rocking back and forth. It was closed with a big padlock. "Agumon, is that you?" Mimi asked.

"Yes!" Agumon yelled as Mimi and Palmon hurried inside.

"Is everyone else with you?" Palmon asked her friend in the locked box.

"We're all here!" Agumon replied.

Mimi kneeled down next to the trunk. "What happened?" she asked.

"We were running from the Numemons," Agumon explained. "Then Monzaemon came along. We ran away from him, but he was too fast for us. And when we fought back, he captured us with his Hearts Attack power!"

"That's terrible," Mimi squealed.

"Yes!" Agumon replied. "And then Monzaemon said that we all had to serve him and his toys now—and that we were going into their new community toy box of children!"

"That's it!" Mimi said. "They're toys for

 75

toys. . . . The toys have been playing with them!"

"Agumon, what changed Monzaemon?" Palmon asked.

"We don't know," Agumon replied.

"Well, can't you get out of that box and help?" Mimi asked.

"We're locked inside, Mimi!" Agumon answered.

"It's up to you two," Gabumon called from inside the locked trunk. "You two must be the heroes this time!"

9

"What do you mean?" Palmon asked.

"You must defeat Monzaemon," Biyomon said firmly through the locked chest.

"What?" Palmon exclaimed.

"You're kidding!" Mimi added.

"We can't get free," Agumon reminded her, "until you save the others!"

Mimi groaned in dismay, shaking her head.

"We have to do this," Palmon told her.

Palmon and Mimi said good-bye to the other Digimons and headed back out onto the streets of Toy Town.

"This isn't good," Palmon said nervously as they wandered between the fancy, Old West–style buildings. "Monzaemon's hearts aren't supposed to attack, only give Heart

Hugs. Those usually give people such a good feeling that it makes them want to help others."

Mimi and Palmon walked back into the main square of the town. As soon as they entered the open plaza, T.K. scampered by. A little yellow toy helicopter kept swooping at his head.

T.K. giggled as he ran from the buzzing helicopter. "You can't catch me!" he cried.

"This is ridiculous," Mimi said.

As soon as T.K. hurried out of the town square, a clanging noise behind Mimi and

Palmon made them jump. They whirled around to see what had made the tinny sound. There was a little toy monkey wobbling back and forth, clanging his cymbals together. It was the same monkey who had been chasing Sora earlier.

Mimi glared at the toy monkey. "Stop that noise!" she ordered it. When the monkey refused to stop, Mimi stomped on him with her pink cowboy boot. "Right now!" she yelled.

The monkey stopped, but the noise led Monzaemon right to them. The giant yellow teddy bear loomed over the town, waddling down the street. "It's a happy day in Toy Town," Monzaemon bellowed. But he didn't look or sound happy at all, even though he was holding a bunch of colorful balloons on strings.

"Oh, no!" Mimi cried.

"I hope you like the balloons!" Monzae-mon thundered.

Monzaemon's routine of saying happy things in a mean way really got on Mimi's nerves. "Hey, Yeti Teddy!" she shouted angrily at the huge Digimon. "Whatever you've done to my friends, fix it now or you'll be in trouble!"

Monzaemon's only reply was to shoot two sizzling laser beams right at Mimi.

With a scream, Mimi and Palmon dashed away.

"This isn't funny!" Mimi shouted as she hurried down the street. "I'm being chased by a giant stuffed bear!"

Monzaemon strode through the pale red smoke that came from the ground he had scorched with his eyebeams. His every step was as big as five of Mimi's or Palmon's, and he quickly caught up. "Now, now," he bel-lowed. "Don't run away from Toy Town!" Then Monzaemon shot more lasers from his eyes, blasting the ground in front of Palmon, churning up even more red smoke.

The horde of Numemons burst through the smoke, with the leader in front of the pack. "I'll save you, sugar plum!" he cried.

Monzaemon growled menacingly when he saw the Numemons were on Mimi's side. But when the Numemons started pelting him with plops of numesludge, his growl became a howl of disgust.

Palmon pointed to the leader of the Numemons. "You turn him down, and he

still helps?" she asked Mimi. Palmon sounded impressed.

"Well, Palmon," Mimi replied. "When you've got it, you've got it—"

Mimi's boast was interrupted by six Numemons suddenly landing in a heap at her feet. One punch from Monzaemon had sent them flying.

"Oh, no!" Mimi cried. "The numesludge isn't working!"

10

With a growl, Monzaemon pulled back his puffy arm and knocked another six Numemons to the ground.

"I can't let them fight alone!" Palmon declared.

As Palmon jumped out into the square to join the Numemons, Mimi squealed, "Palmon, be careful!"

Monzaemon flattened another half-dozen Numemons with his giant furry fist.

Palmon glared up at the enormous teddy bear. "Poison Ivy!" she shouted. Her leafy arms stretched out like vines, extending toward Monzaemon. They twined around his punching arm, holding it still.

But not for long. With a giant heave, Monzaemon pulled the tangling vines off his arm and flung Palmon through the air.

84

Palmon let out a short cry as she landed on the stone street.

Mimi ran to her side. "Palmon, talk to me!" she wailed.

Palmon sat up, blinking. "My Poison Ivy's not strong enough," she said.

"Hearts Attack!" Monzaemon growled. "Those two!" A bunch of blue, heart-shaped bubbles appeared in the air. They wiggled and wobbled like gelatin. The gummy hearts zoomed toward Mimi and Palmon.

Mimi screamed and pulled Palmon off the ground. They scrambled out of the way of the attacking hearts.

Suddenly, all the Numemons gathered together and built a living wall in front of the hearts, blocking them from Mimi and Palmon. As the Hearts Attack hit them, the Numemons became trapped inside the bobbing bubbles.

"The Numemons saved us again!" Mimi exclaimed.

Palmon twirled her leafy hands into fists. "Time to take it to the next level," she said. "I may be a lady, but I'm not a pushover!" She snarled with determination. "Time to show this Digimon some manners! Palmon digivolve to . . . Togemon!"

The entire DigiWorld shuddered. Whorls of digital symbols split the air, and Palmon was surrounded by a swarm of energy. Her onion-shaped body swelled as she transformed into a giant spiny barrel cactus.

Huge boxing gloves covered her hands, and a shock of bright orange hair sprang out of the top of her head.

Mimi gasped in awe at her little Digimon's amazing change. Togemon was nearly as tall as Monzaemon!

"You're going down, big boy!" Togemon swore to Monzaemon. "Want to dance with me?"

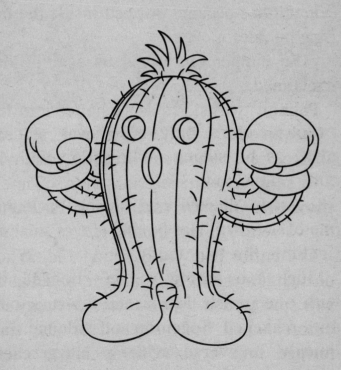

Monzaemon's only reply was a nasty growl as he swung at Togemon with his puffy yellow paw.

Togemon ducked and swung back with one of her own. Her boxing gloves smacked right into the giant teddy.

Much too strong to be knocked out with one punch, Monzaemon struck back and whacked Togemon off-balance. She quickly recovered with a stagger, and fought back with her own gloved fists.

Just as Monzaemon's eyes began to glow, ready to shoot laser beams at Togemon, she took a step backward. "Digimon Needle Spray!" Togemon shouted. All the needles on her body sprang out and sailed at Monzaemon.

Monzaemon howled as his stuffed body was hit by the force. He fell to the ground, and landed with a loud thud. A Black Gear slipped out of the enormous zipper on his back.

The Black Gear spun for a moment in the sky, and then shattered into confetti before it vanished.

Togemon digivolved back to Palmon again. She collapsed at Mimi's feet, completely exhausted.

Mimi bent down and hugged her courageous friend. "Palmon!" she exclaimed with a giggle. "You're fabulous!"

After the Black Gear had disappeared, Monzaemon completely recovered. He was terribly apologetic about his behavior, and he quickly freed the kids from their zombie-like spell, let the Digimons out of the locked trunk, and popped the Hearts Attack bubbles that had captured the Numemons.

Then the giant teddy bear sat down in the middle of the town square, and everybody gathered around him. "When kids get tired of their toys, they just abandon them—throw them away," Monzaemon began. His voice sounded much nicer now. "It's so sad. So, I created a home for these toys." He gestured at the helicopter, wind-up car, and toy bird by his side. "Then I wanted to do all I could to make the toys seem more important to their owners," Monzaemon continued, "by finding a way to let the owners walk in their toys' shoes—"

"By turning kids into zombies?" Mimi interrupted.

"I don't think he really intended to do that, Mimi," Joe told her.

"You're right, Joe," Monzaemon said. "I didn't mean for that to happen. I really am sorry."

 91

Tai laughed. "We know you didn't mean to hurt us," he said.

"I didn't," Monzaemon assured him. "It's just that an evil feeling came over me."

Sora smacked a fist in her other hand. "It was the Black Gear!" she said.

"I'm beginning to take this Black Gear thing a little personally," Tai added. "They cause a whole lot of trouble before disappearing."

"My friends," Monzaemon announced. "Let me show my thanks by giving you a real Heart Hug!"

"Oh, boy," Patamon said, fluttering his wings.

"Watch carefully," Monzaemon said as he climbed to his feet. "This is what it's supposed to be like. Hearts Attack!" he shouted. "With a hug!"

This time, the bubble hearts that appeared

in front of Monzaemon were bright pink. They floated gently down toward the kids and the Digimons, picking each of them up in a protective heart-shaped cocoon that bobbed calmly in the air.

"Oh!" Mimi said as a happy warm feeling flooded her. She giggled as the heart's amazing energy made her entire body tingle with joy.

Giggles rose all around her from the other kids and Digimons as they hovered happily inside their pink hearts.

The leader of the Numemons popped up from a sewer manhole underneath Mimi's bubble. "Dumpling, a kiss for your hero?" he begged her.

Mimi smiled at him. "No," she chirped.

"So feisty!" the slimy leader exclaimed. "What a girl! She'll come around!" He disappeared back down the manhole.

All the kids and the Digimons laughed blissfully as they floated in their wonderful heart bubbles above the streets of Toy Town.